ZIMANI'S DRUM

Liwiro la M'mchenga, mumayambira pamodzi.
Everyone's equal at the start of a race in the sand.
—Malawian proverb

For Bradley, Mike, and Kali
       —M. L.

For Michael Harrison, who plays the world like a drum
       —C. R.

Zimani's Drum is based on "The Blind Man and the Hunchback" from *Some Folk-lore Stories and Songs in Chinyanja* by Robert Sutherland Rattray. London: The Society for Promoting Christian Knowledge, 1907. The song fragment is from the same source. The tale and song are from the Malawi culture of the country of Malawi.

Published by Troll Communications L.L.C.

Published by arrangement with The Rourke Press, Inc.

First paperback edition published 1999.   ISBN 0-8167-6323-2

Printed in the United States of America.

10 9 8 7 6 5 4 3 2 1

PRONUNCIATION AND DEFINITION GUIDE

choinjoli (CHOH in JOH lee): a large drum of East Africa.
Chinyanja (Chin YAN zah): a language of Malawi.
Chichewa (Chi CHEE wa): a language of Malawi.
Lake Nyasa (Nie AH sa): a large lake in East Africa.
Malawi (Meh LAW wee): a country and culture of East Africa.
Mkango (M KAN go): the Chinyanjan word for "lion."
Mlomba (M LOHM bah): a legendary Malawian chief.

The Malawian names in the story are Zimani (Zee MAH nee), Cikungwa (See KUNG wa), Mbudzi (M BUD zee), and Nyango (Nie AN go).

ZIMANI'S DRUM

A Malawian Legend

Retold by
Melinda Lilly

Illustrated by
Charles Reasoner

Troll

Zimani was blind, but he easily made his way along the trail, guided by the *ba-dum ba-dum* of his brother's drumming. He stepped with the beat, resting one hand on his own drum and the other on the shoulder of his brother, Cikungwa. Together they moved as one up the hillside.

The brothers had traveled this path many times before as they went to drum for the villagers around Lake Nyasa. Zimani didn't need his eyesight to find the way. His feet remembered where the soil of the path had worn to rock and where the loose dirt shifted beneath his sandals. He ran his hand along his drum strap and tapped the drum, mimicking his sandals slapping on the hard dirt: *Thunk-a thunk-a.*

"Zimani, your drum helps me hear things I don't usually notice. Your sandals make a rhythm I didn't hear before." Cikungwa's fingers walked on his drum as his feet walked on the pebbles: *Tip-tip.*

"Brother, your drum tells me what you see," said Zimani, following the sound as he trod across the pebbles. "When I hear your drum, I see through your eyes."

4

The rainy season had ended, and the air was heavy with the sweet smells of the grasslands. Zimani recognized the dry scent of a fever tree, remembering the feel of its thorns and featherlike flowers. "What color are the flowers on that fever tree?" he asked.

"Yellow," replied Cikungwa.

Zimani imagined yellow as the sound he made when he brushed his palms across the drum: *Thoo-ey.*

A hot breeze stirred the air, bringing with it a musty smell Zimani also recognized. He imagined the color gold as that smell. "Cikungwa, I smell Lion," he said.

Baboons chattered as the boys hurried into the palm forest. Zimani stood still, breathing hard. "I don't smell it now, do you?"

"No," said Cikungwa, glancing around.

"I think we've left Lion behind," added Zimani hopefully.

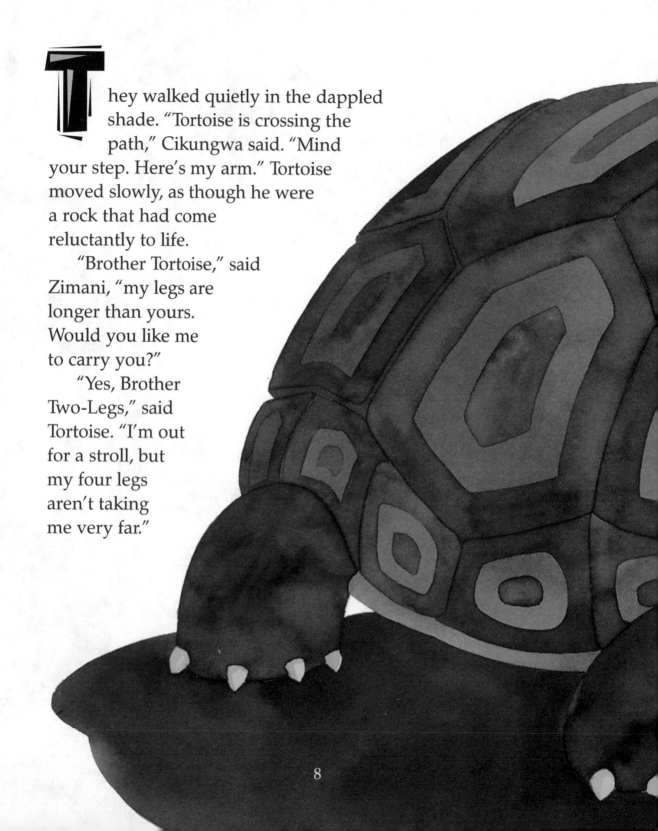

They walked quietly in the dappled shade. "Tortoise is crossing the path," Cikungwa said. "Mind your step. Here's my arm." Tortoise moved slowly, as though he were a rock that had come reluctantly to life.

"Brother Tortoise," said Zimani, "my legs are longer than yours. Would you like me to carry you?"

"Yes, Brother Two-Legs," said Tortoise. "I'm out for a stroll, but my four legs aren't taking me very far."

Zimani bent down and opened his net
bag. Tortoise crawled inside, saying,
"Could you scratch my back? I've
got a tickle." Zimani scratched
Tortoise's shell: *Chka chka*.

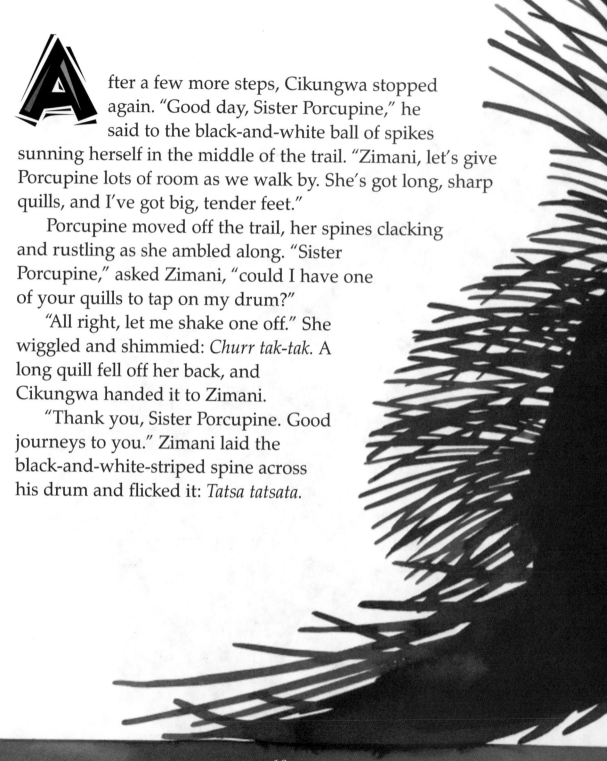

After a few more steps, Cikungwa stopped again. "Good day, Sister Porcupine," he said to the black-and-white ball of spikes sunning herself in the middle of the trail. "Zimani, let's give Porcupine lots of room as we walk by. She's got long, sharp quills, and I've got big, tender feet."

Porcupine moved off the trail, her spines clacking and rustling as she ambled along. "Sister Porcupine," asked Zimani, "could I have one of your quills to tap on my drum?"

"All right, let me shake one off." She wiggled and shimmied: *Churr tak-tak.* A long quill fell off her back, and Cikungwa handed it to Zimani.

"Thank you, Sister Porcupine. Good journeys to you." Zimani laid the black-and-white-striped spine across his drum and flicked it: *Tatsa tatsata.*

Birds sang as the brothers left the forest and entered a dry riverbed: *Towhee dit-dit-dit*. Zimani's and Cikungwa's fingers drummed like birds singing: *Towhee dit-dit-dit*.

Lion roared in the distance: *Ru ru rowRror*.

The brothers' fingers were stiff with fear as they tried to roar with their drums: *Ru-ru-ru*.

"Can't roar like Lion," said Zimani sadly. They stilled their drums and listened for Lion as they walked. The dried mud cracked under their dusty feet. Its parched brittleness reminded Zimani of the time he touched one of the elephant bones littering the riverbed.

His brother took him by the hands, placing Zimani's palms on something cool and smooth: an ivory tusk. Zimani ran his fingers along its length. It was almost as long as his younger brother was tall. Zimani pressed his ear against it. He sensed an old elephant's slow steps—the elephant dead now, but the rhythm still alive in the tusk: *Rumbo ta rum.*

The boys lifted the long tusk on their shoulders and hiked out of the riverbed: *Rumbo ta rum.* "There are fresh lion tracks here," Cikungwa said, picking up the pace.

Soon the brothers passed over a grassy ridge. They heard the high, clear, sweet sound of girls singing from a lone hut in the valley below. Forgetting about Lion for a moment, they stopped and listened to the soaring voices.

Ng'oma ikalira,
Imtenga choinjoli.
When the drum sounds,
The choinjoli drum brings the spirit:
Da brum! Da brum brum brum—

The song was broken by the deafening roar
of Lion close by.

The brothers ran, stumbling and breathless, to the thatched hut of the singers. The door swung inward. "Hurry, come in," said a young girl, helping the brothers inside. "Lion's been circling the house for two days. We were hoping warriors would hear us. But you—"

"We're both too young to carry spears. And I'll never be a warrior," Zimani said evenly.

"I'll never be allowed to be a warrior, either," said the girl softly, grasping Zimani's hand and leading him to a chair. "I'm Mbudzi, and this is my big sister, Nyango."

"We're Zimani and Cikungwa of Mlomba's village. We were on our way to Lake Nyasa to drum," explained Zimani.

"And I am Mkango," snarled Lion, scratching at the cane door.

"Go away! We're not afraid of you!" said Zimani, trying to sound calm. He could hear the door rattling.

"Everyone fears me," Mkango growled, scratching his head. "I am so fierce that when you see the size of the flea that lives in my mane, you'll even be scared of it! But I'm so brave I've barely noticed it." He scratched the biggest of the fleas that had been biting him all day and flicked it under the door.

Zimani was unimpressed to hear the flea scuttle across the floor. "That little nit?" he scoffed, pretending to see it. "Wait until you see the bug that's been on me! My skin is so rough that the pest broke its teeth when it tried to bite me." He whispered to Tortoise, "Friend, lions don't eat you, and you look like a beetle. Do you think you can fool him?" Tortoise crawled out of the hut.

Wide-eyed, Mkango went into an itching fit when he saw the tortoise-bug. As he scratched, he pulled a long strand of hair from his mane. He checked its length and toughness. "One hair from my mighty mane's stronger than the sturdiest vine," he boasted, poking the hair under the door. "Look at it and shake with fear!"

Zimani wasn't scared to hear the gentle *scritch-scritch* sound as the strand was pushed into the hut. "Fine as baby hair," he said with a laugh. "Now let me show you a strong strand of hair." He pushed the porcupine quill outside. "You see my hair?" he asked, nearly believing himself.

Mkango backed up, gasping at the enormous size and sharpness of the strand. "I'll show you!" he yelled, charging the door and clawing a hole in the canes. "I'm famous for my claws. Look how long and sharp they are!"

Zimani slid the elephant's tusk through the hole that Lion had made, saying, "Here's a trimming from the nail on my little finger."

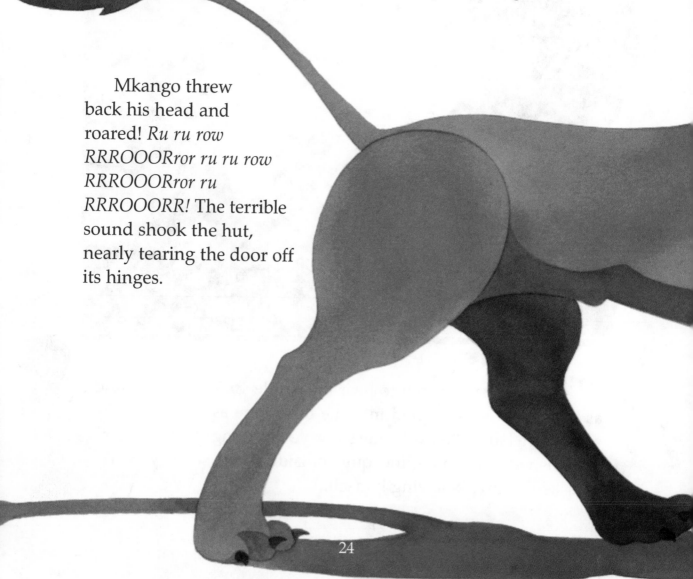

Mkango threw back his head and roared! *Ru ru row RRROOORror ru ru row RRROOORror ru RRROOORR!* The terrible sound shook the hut, nearly tearing the door off its hinges.

Zimani grabbed his drum, beating it with the fury of a warrior! *Ru ru row RRROOORror ru ru row RRROOORror ru RRROOORR!*

Cikungwa grabbed his drum. The brothers pounded the sound of thunder! *Krrrrr KR-KRICH KRAAAKKK!*

The sisters clapped, stomped, and sang with the mighty drums, the noise so loud it shook the skies. *AWW-WEEE KA KRA KRAAAKKK!*

Terrified, Mkango ran away from the sound. He ran over the first hill and then the next. He ran farther and farther, but the mighty drumming still pounded in his ears. He ran over mountains. He swam through rivers. He went so far he never returned to that part of the world.

Zimani and Cikungwa drummed the sound of celebration: *Ta-tutsa ba brum ba braw!* The sisters sang and stomped the dance of joy: *Aww lululu thaw-brum ti-brum!* Celebration and joy echoed around them and in them and never sank into silence.

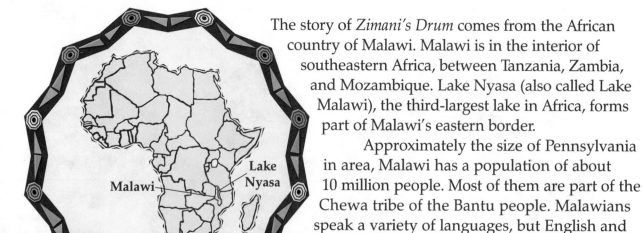

The story of *Zimani's Drum* comes from the African country of Malawi. Malawi is in the interior of southeastern Africa, between Tanzania, Zambia, and Mozambique. Lake Nyasa (also called Lake Malawi), the third-largest lake in Africa, forms part of Malawi's eastern border.

Approximately the size of Pennsylvania in area, Malawi has a population of about 10 million people. Most of them are part of the Chewa tribe of the Bantu people. Malawians speak a variety of languages, but English and Chichewa (the language of the Chewa) are the two official languages.

In the 1400s, Malawi was a part of the mighty Maravi kingdom. At its strongest, the Maravi kingdom stretched as far south as Zimbabwe, hundreds of miles from Lake Nyasa. After two hundred years, however, the kingdom began to crumble, mainly due to local wars and the slave trade.

In 1859, the famous British explorer and missionary David Livingstone arrived in Malawi. Eventually, the British claimed Malawi as a *protectorate*— a dependent political unit—named Nyasaland. After independence in 1964, Malawi adopted its present name.

Malawi is one of the poorest countries in the world, with very little manufacturing or mining to provide income for its people. The chief products are agricultural, primarily tea, tobacco, and sugar.

Malawi is a beautiful country, however, with stunning landscapes. The tropical climate includes a dry season from May to November and a rainy season from November to May. There are large expanses of grassland and mountains covered with forests. Five national parks protect the wild animals that roam there, such as elephants, lions, leopards, and antelopes. The country also has a rich culture of dance, storytelling, and music— especially drumming.